Darkest DESIRES

NEW YORK TIMES & USA TODAY BESTSELLING AUTHOR

NICOLE BLANCHARD

Dedication

If you'd kneel for a stranger in a mask, this is for you

Contents

I delete another text from my ex-boyfriend and manage to feel only the slightest twinge of guilt. It's not his fault I broke up with him, but the least I can do is not lead him on anymore. Much as I enjoyed his charm and sense of humor, those just aren't the qualities in a man that get me off.

My tastes are much more...complicated.

And much more than a pretty little frat boy like him could ever manage to handle.

I sigh and crank up the A/C on my ten-year-old sedan, crossing my fingers it'll be able to make it the remaining twenty miles to Nassau, Florida, my hometown. Nothing like limping back home with no job, no apartment, and no love life to speak of.

Apparently, the bigger your dreams, the harder

you fall when they don't come true. Considering I'll be bunking with my mom for the foreseeable future I'll officially consider this move the splat on the ground I've been waiting for. Definitely not the star of Broadway like I'd always dreamed.

My phone buzzes and I snatch it up from the center console to give the pretty little frat boy a firm fuck off, when I recognize my mom's name on the caller I.D. I smother a groan.

"No, I'm not there yet," I answer without preamble.

"Well, considering that I'm sitting in the living room and you're not here, I'm not surprised, but that's not why I called." Even though my crushing failure in New York hasn't given me much to smile about, the sound of my mother's Southern twang brings one to my lips.

I flick on my blinker and take the exit to Nassau. Dread settles low in my stomach. I blow out a series of short breaths. Would moving back home be just another on my list of failures? Brushing those doubts away, I say, "Then why did you call?"

She murmurs to someone else in the room and then fumbles the phone. "Sorry, had to let Fifi in. Anyway, what was I saying?"

Only half paying attention to her, I merge with traffic. "Well, you haven't really said anything yet."

"Oh!" she exclaims. I hold the phone away from my ear at the increase in volume. "I remember. Well you know Jennifer, from work?" She doesn't pause for my response before continuing. Her rambles are often one-sided so I reapply my lip gloss as I wait at a stop sign. "She was telling me yesterday about this new ER doc on the floor. He's about your age, maybe a little older. Handsome. *Single.* Apparently, he just so happens to love theatre." Her smug tone is apparent even over the spotty cell phone connection.

Scowling at my flushed expression in the rearview mirror, I find myself considering her news. I don't know if I'm embarrassed because I have to resort to my mom choosing my dates, intrigued because: doctor, single, theatre lover, or if I'm just plain tired of the whole dating game. I forego all three and just go to my default setting: dismissive. "Please tell me you aren't trying to set me up."

"It's not a setup, I'm just *saying.*" If I know my mother, I know she's smiling now as well as smug.

"You're meddling."

"I can't help it. It's what I'm supposed to do."

"I'm starting to regret moving back already and I haven't even gotten there yet."

"You won't regret it," she says. "We're going to have so much fun. We can go out to dinner, see movies. Oh, I know! There's a new club that just opened up that I've just been dying to try."

Her enthusiasm is catching, and I smile. At least one thing about moving back won't completely suck. "Your social life sounds more exciting than mine."

"We'll just have to get you out of the house," she says. "Maybe you should meet this doctor," she adds nonchalantly.

Intuition prickles and I groan. "You set me up, didn't you?"

There's a telling pause before she says, "I may have mentioned your name to Jennifer to pass on in case he was interested." Another heavy pause. "Then, I may have convinced him to take you to dinner."

I groan. "Mom."

"Stella," she mocks.

"I haven't even been here a day and you're already interfering in my personal life."

"I don't consider it interfering if the end result is good for you."

Tilting my head to the side, I change the radio stations, lowering the volume so I can concentrate on her words. "I guess I don't have much else to do when I get there."

She squeals. "You won't regret it. He is H-O-T, hot."

"I don't think you're supposed to talk about your coworkers like that. I'm pretty sure there are seminars about it."

"Trust me. When you meet him you'll understand."

Sighing, I say, "Well when am I supposed to meet this illustrious doctor? If he's not as extraordinary as you're making him out to be, you owe me a bottle of wine—and not the cheap stuff either!"

"If you like him, you owe *me* two grandbabies, at least. One boy and one girl. You don't have to name them after me, but under no circumstances are they allowed to call me grandma. I'm Nana."

"Geez, he must be something else if you're advocating the white picket fence and happily ever afters." As a notorious bachelorette, Mom had never been married. I don't think she'd ever had a boyfriend for longer than a menstrual cycle. She's more relationship phobic than I am.

"I'm not saying you have to marry the guy for Christ's sake. I'm just saying if I were twenty years younger, I'd give him a roll in the sheets."

"I just got *out* of a relationship in case you've forgotten already."

"Sure, with what's-his-name. But that's beside the point."

"Fine. When am I supposed to meet him, then?"

"Tonight."

Dead air fills the line between us. I gawk at the cars in front of me. She can't be serious. "Tonight?"

"Well, I felt bad that I have a night shift and I didn't want you to spend your first night home all alone and depressed, getting into my ice cream stash."

"I'm not going to eat all of your ice cream," I sputter.

"That's what you said the last time you came home," she says.

"I can't decide if I should be upset because you set me up without asking or because you did it to keep me from raiding your freezer."

"You can *thank me* for it later. You're meeting him tonight at seven at *Bella Bella Italiano*. Dress nice," she says cheerfully, then hangs up without letting me have a word in edgewise.

The balmy night air wraps around my bare legs and I give a fleeting thought to whether or not a form fitting little black dress is appropriate for a blind date. Then, I figure, screw it. I look spectacular in this dress. And I could use a little more feeling spectacular and a lot less of feeling like a failure.

I'm a fifteen minutes early, but I couldn't stand being alone in the house surrounded by the corpses of empty boxes and realizing just how far I'd fallen. Meeting a good looking guy to take my mind off of unpacking the rest of my meager belongings started to sound better around the time I found the box full of relics from my failed relationship.

The hostess greets me with a wide smile that I mimic in return. "How many?" she asks, and I wonder why that should feel like a bullet to the gut when I've never had a problem being alone before.

"I'm here to meet someone," I say to cover my sudden and rare bout of insecurity. "I'm a little early. Will it be alright if I just wait at the bar until they get here?"

She nods, "Absolutely. What's the name? I'll let them know you've already arrived."

"Mikhail, uh...Alexandrov," I say, wincing when I mangle the pronunciation horribly. "Dr. Mikhail Alexandrov."

"I'll let him know. Go right on in to your left." Her

Southern twang and hospitality a welcome reprieve from the often rude New Yorkers.

The interior is dimly lit and shadowed, the air scented heavily with garlic and oregano. My stomach growls, reminding me I didn't put food on the list of priorities when I got to Mom's house. As much as I protested, the thought of a date buoyed my mood and meant the two hours between pulling into her drive and leaving for the restaurant were spent primping and beautifying—two of my favorite activities.

It's worth it. My long brown hair is styled into artful waves. I applied makeup with a slight hand, having grown tired of thick applications after one too many stage performances. Now, I tend to go for a more natural look. A little liner to emphasize my sultry brown eyes and a light gloss on my full lips. The result is sexy casual and I'm aware enough of myself to recognize the blatant interest on the faces of men stealing not-so-subtle glances as I make my way to the bar.

"White wine," I tell the bartender as I take a seat on one of the empty stools.

As he sets the chilled glass in front of me, I take it with a grateful smile. My hands tremble a little as I bring the wine glass to my lips and I hope the preemptive glass of alcohol will help settle my nerves.

My phone buzzes and I dig through my purse,

knocking it from the bar to the floor with a muttered, "Shit," when a group of people pass by. The hushed tones of their conversation filter over the piano music and chatter from the other patrons.

I completely forget the phone, the text most likely from my ex, and my blind date when I hear one woman say, "I'm not so sure about this corset I just ordered. Do you prefer the ones with plastic boning or steel?"

"Honestly, the stronger the better, in my opinion, so mine are all made with steel."

"Well, I ordered one of each, so I guess we'll see. I'll wear it the next time I go to the club and let you see."

"You better. Corsets are a fetish of mine." The woman's laughter is warm and throaty. She and her companion are passing by the bar toward a secluded room in the back where more people have gathered.

I imagine wearing a leather corset, maybe the one I wore underneath my costume for my last period performance. Except this time, I don't have anything on over top of it. All eyes are on me. My skin prickles as I picture the scene and get to my feet. I down the rest of my wine in a couple gulps to cool the rising heat in my body. If anything, the alcohol is kindling to flame, making me burn brighter.

I shift from foot to foot, feeling more anxious, elated and apprehensive than I did at my first stage performance. I'd heard of people who were into fetish things—you can't really live in New York and not meet some characters, but aside from porn and books, I'd never met someone who seemed so open about it.

And in Nassau of all places.

I should sit down, order another glass, and wait for my date's arrival. I should, but even as I waver on the brink of indecision, my feet are already moving.

Leaving the empty glass on the bar, I follow the women down the shadowed hall on the pretense of finding the bathroom. At least that's what my excuse will be if they catch me. My intense yearning for something I don't quite understand doesn't give a damn about propriety as I tilt an ear to listen to the rest of their low conversation.

"Did you try the new knotted flogger they have at *Risky Business*?" The woman who laughed shivers now as if recalling the pleasurable act. My heart starts to race.

"No, girl. I stick to the deerskin. I haven't quite graduated to the rougher stuff yet."

"You don't know what you're missing."

"Well, maybe next time."

They reach the entrance to the room and the first

woman turns to the other, then notices me in the background. "Sorry," she says as she holds the door open for her companion. "Didn't see you there. Are you here for the munch?" she asks. At my confused stare, she adds, "Ah. You must be a first timer. Don't worry, we don't bite. Unless you're into that sort of thing." She widens the door and holds open a hand. "C'mon, don't be shy."

Laughter explodes from inside the room and I catch phrases that cause my stomach muscles to tense. Master. Slave. Beg. Come. Need. Take.

Teetering on the precipice of all the yearnings I've suppressed, I take her hand and enter the room.

2

The room narrows in the shadows, a roaring in my ears blots out the hushed conversation from the restaurant behind me. Thankful for the darkness that covers my blush, I say, "I'm sorry, I don't think I was invited," as I step through the threshold. "I'll just go."

She waves my hesitation away with one elegant hand. "Nonsense. I can tell a like-minded individual when I see one. Why don't you stick around for the munch? No strings. If it's not your thing you can leave, no hard feelings."

"I don't—" I take a deep breath, soothe my already jangled nerves, and paste on a confused smile. "Lunch? Bit late for that, isn't it?"

"Aren't you cute?" she says with a smile. "Munch."

Even though I've spent the better part of my twenties in one of the trendiest cities in the world, I find myself grasping at memories, wondering if I missed some important social convention. Finally, I say, "I'm not sure what a munch is, exactly."

"Nothing serious," she assures me. "Just a gathering for folks in the lifestyle. Food. Wine. Conversation."

"Lifestyle," I say with a twinge, okay more than a twinge, of curiosity.

"BDSM," she says, her eyes twinkling. "A much is just a get together for those in the lifestyle to socialize. They're mostly meant for those who are curious about BDSM to talk with others, get comfortable. We meet here and a couple other local restaurants so those interested in joining can get their feet wet, learn about The Sanctum, and get comfortable. We share stories, gossip, and enjoy some great food and company."

I nod, but she's already flitting off to socialize with the rest of the people in the room. They don't look particularly 'different', though there are some with a predilection for leather attire, but it's subtle. Knee-high leather boots with kickass skinny jeans, genuine belts, vests. Chokers also seem to be a theme, again subtly. If the woman hadn't pointed out it was a BDSM meeting, I wouldn't have noticed. Then I remember the word *slave* I'd heard early and can't help the blood that rushes to my cheeks.

"Are you new here?" comes a smooth voice.

Turning, I find a reasonably attractive, well-dressed man in his mid to late thirties. He doesn't look like he'd be the type of man to frequent what I imagine to be a dungeon-esque club, wielding whips or belts or other whatever-the-hell. My flair for the dramatic leads me to imagine him surrounded by a wall of red velvet with black tools hanging on hooks.

My lips curve in a natural response to the attention. "I guess you can say that."

"Are you a friend of Tally's?" he says, nodding toward the woman I was speaking with. So that was her name.

Shaking my head, I say, "No, we just met. I've never been to one of these things before."

"Would you like to—"

My phone buzzes in my purse and I give the man an apologetic smile. "I really apologize, normally I wouldn't be so impolite as to answer a phone like this, but I was supposed to meet someone before I came here."

He nods. "Of course. It was nice to meet you..."

"Stella," I supply, then take a few steps away toward a secluded corner, pulling my phone from my purse. I'd nearly forgotten about my blind date and guilt settles low in my stomach.

Even a momentary brush with this new, dark, and needy flavor of sex has my blood thrumming hot in my veins. It has my mouth going dry, so I'm thankful when I realize it's a text and not a phone call. I put in my code and navigate to my text messages.

> Mikhail: Stella, I hate to get off on the wrong foot before we've even first met, but we'll have to reschedule today. I've had an emergency with a patient and can't get away. Are you free Saturday? Your mother mentioned you like the theatre. I have box tickets.

Somewhat relieved and disappointed, I tap out:

> That sounds wonderful. Just let me know what time and where.

I wander back to the crowd of people, feeling more in my element now that I don't have to worry about being caught by one of my mom's coworkers at a meeting for a sex club. When I get another text, I glance at it, perhaps a little too eagerly, and I'm sorely disappointed when I realize its from my ex.

The waiter comes then and I order a grilled chicken salad with another glass of wine. I don't want to get drunk, but I definitely need the social lubrication. He brings the wine immediately and I gulp half of it down within seconds.

Tension grows between my shoulders, locking me up tight. What the hell am I doing here with these strangers? I have to be some sort of fucked up to be excited by it. By the prospect of going to a club like this. And, God, do I want to. Based on the topics floating around, I've only scratched the surface of all the kinds of sex and kink possible.

I don't know whether I should be turned on by those possibilities...or running in the other direction.

Natural gravity, or perhaps orchestration, has me sitting between the woman, Tally, and the man I'd spoken with before. Around me, conversation flows and is as diverse as the participants. It volleys from the newest and most effective methods of spanking, to retirement funds, and tax preparations. Much as I'm used to crowds, even I become overwhelmed by the rapid-fire change in subjects.

"You don't strike me as a submissive," says the man next to me, his eyes warm, but inquisitive. "What exactly is your kink?"

I take a sip of my wine before answering. "To be honest, I'm not really sure," I tell him in a stage whisper.

With amused interest, he says, "Never been to a club like this before?"

"I'm going to show my naiveté, but to be honest I'm still not sure what this club is exactly."

He leans back in his seat, taking a drink from his own short glass of amber liquid. "I think you know more than you think."

"Whips and chains," I say offhandedly. A joke, but I think we both know I'm not really joking.

He winks. "And more. But I don't think you're into that so much."

Fascinated, I lean an elbow on the table and prop my chin in my hand. "How can you tell?"

"Well for one, you don't have a problem looking me in the eye. In fact, you seem more concerned about how other people are looking at *you*." He pauses, before his smile turns rueful. "Mores the pity. I'd love to get my hands on you."

Glancing down at my plate of untouched chicken salad, I remind myself these people deal with discerning wants and desires from everyone they interact with. Unused to the scrutiny, I fidget in my seat, toying with my fork. "I guess you can say I enjoy the spotlight. I was an actress."

"Was?"

See? Discerning. "I just recently moved back to the area from New York."

"Ah," he says knowingly. "Now it makes sense."

Frowning, I say, "Excuse me?"

Before he can respond, the dinner comes to an end, and the others start getting to their feet. Standing, I polish off my glass of wine, my head spinning more from the sudden turn of events than the alcohol, and I push in my chair. What had he learned about me in such a short conversation that I hadn't been able to figure out in twenty-four years?

"You should come on Friday," he says as he helps me from my chair.

"What's on Friday?" I ask. The words slip from my lips before I can choke them back. What am I doing?

"Guests are allowed to come to the club. Take a look around. I think you'd enjoy it."

"I'll consider it," I say with a smile. "It was nice talking to you," I add.

"You too."

As I walk out the door, the woman who extended the invitation smiles warmly. "If you are interested, we welcome you to join us the day after tomorrow. We open the club to guests. It'll be somewhat like today, unless you'd like to take it further. The man you were speaking with can serve as your reference when the hostess asks."

Not trusting myself to comment, afraid I'll blurt out my eagerness and embarrass myself, I nod and accept the card she extends.

Filing out after the rest of the crowd, I fumble with my purse, stuffing the card inside and pulling out my phone to keep my hands busy. If living in New York for the past four years had taught me anything, it was how to look busy and important in any social situation.

The phone rings in my hands as I walk out the front door of the restaurant and head to my car. Glancing at the caller I.D., my stomach flips a little when I recognize Mikhail's number.

"Hello," he says.

Needing the solitude, I duck into my car. I clear my throat and respond breezily, "You better not be calling to cancel again."

An undeniably male chuckle washes over me like silk, turning my already heated blood molten from the sound alone. Clearly, I needed to get laid, or invest in some sort of battery-operated relief. My eyes catch on the white outline of the card in the darkness.

His voice distracts me from an imagination fraught with images of The Sanctum. "Not a chance," he says. "I hope I didn't ruin your first night back."

Already knowing I won't be able to resist the invitation to their guest night, I bite my lip to contain the hum of anticipation that bubbles up in my throat, then focus on my response to Mikhail. "Is it rude if I say no? It was a great restaurant. Good choice. Would have been better with your company, but I managed to enjoy myself."

"Glad to hear it." In the background, I note the low murmur from the radio, then the silence from his engine turning off, followed by two beeps from his car. I try to imagine him based on the sound of his voice alone. Mom mentioned he's good looking. As I conjure an image of a tall, broad man cloaked in shadows, he says, "Does six work for you Saturday?"

"It does," I say as I start my own car and pull into traffic for the short ride home.

He yawns heavily into the phone, and then laughs at himself. "I don't make a habit of cancelling on beautiful women, then boring them to death."

Feeling more at ease, I join him in laughter. "Long day?"

"The longest." His groan is deep and conjures even more heated images.

God. I flick on the air conditioning, hoping it will help alleviate the scalding lust inside of me.

"Epsom salts," I suggest after a few seconds. "Mom always says they work wonders after a long shift."

"Am I that transparent?"

"Yes," I say bluntly, then we laugh again as I pull

into my drive. "And I've seen it many times before. She always said night shifts were the hardest."

"You don't want to hear about my night," he says over the click of ice in a glass. I picture him pouring a couple fingers of whiskey. He'd be wearing slacks, a crisp, collared shirt unbuttoned at the top, his tie hanging loosely on either side of his neck. "It wasn't one of the good ones."

"Sometimes we need the bad to appreciate the good," I say, still sitting in the quiet dark of my car. The lights inside the house are still out; Mom hasn't made it home yet. Much as I love her, I'm glad. Way too much has happened tonight for me to process without her probing questions added to the mix.

The ice in his drink clicks against the glass and I hear him swallow. "Do you really believe that?" he asks.

"Sometimes." I give a self-depreciating laugh. "Not so much right now, considering I'm couch surfing at my mom's and accepting her advice on my love life. But normally, yes. A year from now, I imagine I'll look back and be grateful for the low points. It's all about perspective, right? Well, at least that's what they say."

"Hard to think that way when you're wrist deep in the stomach of a shooting victim."

Concern softens my response and I wince. "Definitely Epsom salts. Your back must be killing you."

Leather creaks and fabric rustles as he shifts in his seat. My breath catches in my throat as the sounds echo in the closed quarters of my car. "Now that you mention it, yeah. Maybe I should have come to dinner after all. You are a regular fount of information."

"I also give a killer massage," I say.

"Now you're just being cruel," he says in response.

Needing the fresh air to clear my mind and give me a sense of control, I get out of the car and let it wash over my fevered skin. "Did he make it?"

"Barely." There's a pause, then a sigh. "Enough about that. Tell me about you. I'm sure you can't be the angel Diana makes you out to be."

Smiling, I unlock the front door to Mom's house and let myself into the empty living room. "She can't help herself. Since I'm an only child, she's always spoiled me."

"Don't I know it. She knew I wasn't interested in dating and yet, here we are."

I toss my keys on the buffet table next to the front door. "I hope she wasn't too much of a pest."

"Considering I'm getting a massage out of the deal, I'm feeling more into the idea of a blind date. Besides, I always look for an excuse to go to the theatre."

A laugh tickles the back of my throat. "Do you go often?"

"Not as much as I'd like. Work keeps me pretty full up these days. I'm surprised you still like it, even though you're there for work all the time."

"Not so much these days, but I wouldn't have gotten into acting if I didn't love it."

"What do you love about it?"

Settling onto the fluffy couch that has been a staple in our household for as long as I can remember, I stare up at the ceiling, considering. "At first it was just an obligation. You know? School plays, high school performances, speeches. But as I got older, I realized I was good at it. Really good. And I liked being up on stage, feeling almost invincible, being anyone in the world."

"Must be a great feeling, having all those adoring eyes on you."

Laughing softly, I murmur, "Unless you put on a bad performance."

"Well, I doubt you've ever given one."

"Not too many, but everyone has a few." I toe off my shoes and stretch my legs on the cushions.

"If you enjoy it so much, what brings you back to Nassau? As much as I love the arts, we aren't exactly known for them."

Blowing out a breath, I say, "I guess I'm one of the

unlucky thousands with big dreams and not enough talent. After college, New York was all I wanted, all I could think about. Those big dreams died hard when I woke up a couple weeks ago and realized I've been slogging for years without making any headway. I never even landed a real audition. So I gave up my room in the apartment I shared with six other actresses and came home."

"What are you going to do now?"

"Teach acting?" I say with a humorless laugh. "I don't know. Maybe go back to college for something else."

"I'm sure you'll figure it out."

"Thanks. I hope so."

"And you never know." I hear him smiling over the line. "Maybe I'll see you on stage sometime."

The laughter bubbling in my throat spills over my lips. "Want a special performance, huh?" I bite my lip, stemming the flirtatious banter that threatens to burst forth. I haven't even met this guy and I'm already flirting with him. First the club, now this. My sex-drive must be in high gear.

"I wouldn't say no to one," he says, his voice low and inviting.

"Maybe if Saturday goes well, you will."

"Upping the stakes, hmm."

"Incentive," I nearly whisper it over the line. The part inside of me stoked by the thought of the club is enjoying the back and forth with this stranger. Maybe it's easier because I can't see him. Haven't met him. He's still an imaginary lover, practically anyone I want him to be. My ex hadn't been so open to out-right flirtation and he loathed most overtures of a sexual nature. It's no wonder I'd grown stifled in the relationship.

"I'll put my game face on," he says next. "Make sure you wear something that will put your mom to shame for setting us up."

"I don't know, she's a pretty risqué woman herself. It'd take a whole hell of a lot to drop her jaw."

"Even better," he says.

"What are we going to see?"

He tsks. "Now that would ruin the surprise and since I've already gotten off on the wrong foot, I'm going to need all the help I can get."

"I don't know," I murmur. "You seem to be doing just fine on your own." His chuckle makes me squirm on the couch, my legs rubbing against each other as if it'll help burn off the nervous energy pulsing in my veins. "What about you? Did you always want to be a doctor?"

His sigh is long this time, weighted. "Some days I don't even remember why."

"Hard, I imagine."

"It can be."

"I don't know if I could handle that kind of pressure."

"I don't know," he says, "I couldn't imagine being on the stage in front of hundreds of people."

"Totally not the same thing. No one's life depends on me."

Liquid splashes into his glass and the bottle thumps down on the table. "Don't devalue yourself like that. People need entertainment just as much as medicine. I can heal them, bandage their wounds, prescribe them medicine, but I can't make them smile like you. Make them laugh."

His words steal the breath straight from my lungs. Out of all the pieces of advice, words of encouragement, and doling out of sympathy, no one had made me feel quite as good as the comments from a complete stranger.

"Thank you," I say, when I manage to steady my voice enough to respond. "That means a lot to me."

"No matter what you say, going out to follow your dreams is never a mistake and you have more guts than most people for setting out on your own to make them come true."

Blushing and grateful he can't see it, I say, "You're changing the subject."

"Caught," he says without shame. He pauses, then adds, "How about this? I'll let you ask as many questions as you want when I see you on Saturday. Does that work for you?"

"You may end up regretting this," I warn.

"Not a chance," he says, causing my lips to spread into a smile. "I'll call you tomorrow."

1

I've been many people.

A queen. A lover. A daughter. A prostitute.

Even with all the costumes, makeup, and masks I've worn, no amount of stage time or acting lessons could have prepared me for the cascade of fear and uncertainty that rush over me as I pull up to the nondescript building where The Sanctum is located.

I never would have expected a BDSM dungeon to be located on a relatively normal-looking street. The brick building looks like many others surrounding it, right down to the wrought iron balconies and New Orleans style lamps lining the front face. The only oddity is the single front door and the lack of windows on the first two floors.

Guiding my car down the road to find a parking

spot nearby, my stomach tangled in knots, I wonder if I'm making a huge mistake.

Again.

I wish I were the type of person I projected to people. Confidence is easy to emulate and so much harder to actually believe yourself. Nevertheless, I choke back my indecision, fueled by blatant curiosity and growing need.

Like recognizes like. Hadn't Tally mentioned something similar?

Is that why I am so drawn to the idea of this club and the experiences I may have here?

I pull into the parking spot with damp hands clutched on the steering wheel. Feeling rushes back to them as I release the wheel and grab my bag. There wasn't a dress code that I'm aware of, but even so, I wish there was. It would have been a million times easier if they'd given me guidelines, rules. Even as an artist, I can respect rules in this sense, but aside from "Keep your mouth shut", the card doesn't list any other requirements.

I decided to keep it simple and wear a dress similar to the one I wore to the munch. Clingy, black, easy to move in, and attractive. Unsure of what, exactly, I'm going to get into, I figure something easy to take on... and off...is best.

My skin heats as I abscond from the car, my purse shouldered. Cool air winds around my limbs and reminds me of how exposed I am. I shiver as I cross the street to the one and only door. Finding it unlocked, I enter with bated breath.

The foyer doesn't scream sex-club to me. If anything it reminds me of several other restaurants and businesses in Nassau, including *Bella Bella.* Subtly Italian, all dark wood and black and gold accents. Looking around, I note a door to my right partway open. A quick glance inside shows flickering screens and an attentive guard manning a desk covered with papers.

There's another door to the left, one that leads into another shadowed room with more dark wood. Heart racing, hands damp, I delve into the shadows.

A hostess stand is to my immediate right and a smiling woman in a bustier, that leaves little to the imagination, is situated behind it. "Welcome to The Sanctum," she says, smiling.

"Hello," I manage. "I was invited to the guest night. I hope I'm in the right place."

Her smile widens. "You've found it. If you'll please provide your phone—don't worry, you'll get it back at the end of the night. We don't allow any cameras or video equipment to protect the privacy and identities of our patrons."

Wow, really? My surprise must show on my face because she adds, "Most of our members don't like to advertise their membership—for good reason. You're going to run into people from the community and this isn't the kind of club you'd like to advertise to your family members." Her eyes twinkle, "Keep your mouth shut and all."

"I understand," I say as I hand my phone over. She logs it and clicks at her computer.

"Guests are allowed on the first floor. If you'd like to go higher, you'll need to be escorted by a member. Most of the general rules are common sense and you'll see them posted or you may ask a DM—dungeon master—if you have any questions. Just be respectful."

Nodding, I lift my hand when she gestures for it. She takes my pointer finger and presses it against an identifier pad, then keys into the computer again.

"If you do decide to become a member, you'll go through our two owners, Mr. Mak and Ms. Fremanis. If you went to the munch, you've met Tally—Ms. Fremanis." Done with the business on the computer, the hostess smiles again. "Would you like a booth or a spot at the bar?"

"Bar, please. Thank you."

She gestures toward the inside of the club, and I take the first step inside.

Music pulses and colorful strobe lights flicker on my right over a dance floor full of writhing limbs and sweat-slicked skin. To the right of the generous dance floor is a full bar with a smattering of tables situated in front.

I beeline for the bar and order a white wine, gulping it like water when the bartender sets it in front of me. Too much more of this twisted anxiety and desire, and I'm going to turn into a raging alcoholic.

With my wine glass held in front of my chest like a shield, I turn on my mahogany bar stool to survey the rest of The Sanctum. I'm seated on the end corner of the bar, closest to the dance floor. Heat pours off the mass of bodies in waves, and I lift the thick curtain of hair off my neck and let it drape around my shoulder.

On the other side of the dance floor, I can see the tops of a pair of frosted glass doors. Shadows of bodies flit across the surface and V.I.P. is affixed to the front in gold lettering. Opposite the V.I.P. section is a wall of booths. It takes a moment for me to realize the walls between the booths are removable, allowing for larger parties. There's one such party going on at the farthest booth, and features a group of members in various states of undress.

Everywhere I look, I find carnal scenes, making my heart beat fast in my throat. I wipe my palms on the material of my dress and order another white wine. The second glass helps steady my nerves and by the end, I've joined the bodies on the dance floor, enjoying the heavy bass and frenetic pace. Hands and bodies brush against me, so quickly that I can't make out who they belong to.

God, yes. This is exactly what I need. Time to blow off steam. A little fun to forget everything else I'm running away from. A moment of reprieve before I figure out what the hell I'm going to do next.

A pair of strong arms wrap around my waist and large hands coast down my ribs to settle on the flair of my hips. They grip me with reassuring firmness, an anchor in the sea of bodies surrounding us.

I peer through lids, heavily weighted with lust and excitement, to find a couple kissing passionately in front of us. Heat spears through me, violent and true. When the man draws his hands down and under the fluttery edge of my dress, I gulp deep breaths, but can't seem to find my equilibrium.

"Don't think," he whispers, his voice gruff in my ear. His breath tickles, entices, and I shiver against his hard length. "Just feel."

And I do. I feel everything. From the fast racing

pulse of the music, echoed by the thud of my heart-beat, to the searing flush of heat coating my skin, burning me from the inside out, to the raw tease of his whiskers on the curve of my neck. Behind me, his chest is firm and broad. Powerful. Strong. The kind of man who can overtake, overpower, and overwhelm you. I'm instantly, shamelessly wet.

His hands delve higher, teasing the tender flesh of my inner thigh with the tips of his fingers, the edge of his nails. If he goes any higher he'll no doubt find the evidence of my arousal. I refocus on the scene in front of me, trying to gain some handle on the wild spinning room and I notice the couple in front of us is no longer kissing. They're watching, eyes glued to the hand underneath my skirt.

I freeze against the stranger behind me, unsure if I should run to the exit...or let him continue. Based on my body's response, I'd let him do a whole number of things. Anything he wants.

And I want it. Isn't that why I came here? To explore this side of me? The side frantic couplings in the dorms and endless nights of missionary never seemed to satisfy.

"If you're uncomfortable, we can move to a more private booth," he says against my throat, his fingers still teasing my thigh. His voice is low, so low I have to strain to hear him over the pounding music. It's secrets and sin, a dark silk colored with temptation.

The first thing that comes to mind as I worry through my indecision is Mikhail. Which is all sorts of crazy. But his kind voice and troubled conversation was endearing. He's exactly the sort of man I should be going after. A kind man who has his shit together. A good man.

Just when I open my mouth to protest and pull away, the stranger behind me lifts his fingers to the strip of cloth framing my pussy and the words die a pitiful death in my throat. Surrendering, I twine my arms up and around his neck, pulling his warmth closer to my back. The woman in front of me smiles encouragingly, as both she and her partner watch the stranger's hands play underneath my dress.

"Do you want me to make you come?" he asks, his deft fingers slipping underneath the edge of my panties.

My legs tighten around his wrist reflexively to keep from melting to the floor. His free arm wraps around my waist to keep me standing. Barely.

"Here?" I don't know if I'd rather he whisked me away to a secluded corner, or if I want the anonymous couple in front of us to witness the erotic display. I've always loved being on stage, performing, but this takes it to the extreme.

"If you want." His fingers trace through my wetness. "We can stay right here. Let them see you." When I don't say anything, he continues, "You aren't attached to anyone, are you?"

"No," I manage, licking my lips and breathing heavily. Just hearing the word from his mouth is enough to make the word a moan. *Master*.

The fingers around my waist flex, and he exhales. "Would you like to be mine for the night?"

My pussy ripples with need, achingly empty. When I manage to speak, my voice cracks, which shocks the hell out of me. Thousands of performances. Speeches. Do-or-die auditions and I've never fumbled a line. Missed a mark. But one touch from this mystery man and I'm damn near struck senseless. At a loss for words. "I'm not s-sure exactly what that means. This is my first time here. Doing anything like this."

"It means you let me decide what you want, because I'll give it to you. It's my responsibility to learn what you like. What drives you." He slips a finger into me, wrenching a broken gasp from my throat. Working it in and out of my tightness, his voice grows gravely. "What excites you. What makes you come undone."

My hand grips his around my waist. "You mean things like this?"

He drapes my hair over my shoulder so his lips can press against my neck. "Yes, and other things."

Images flash like quicksilver through my mind. "Like what? You want to hurt me? I'm not so sure I'm into pain."

"I'm only interested in your pleasure," he says. "And we'll discuss any particulars if you're interested in doing a scene in one of the private rooms." The couple in front of us still watches with hungry eyes. His fingers are moving more insistently now, urgently, inside me. "I would never do anything you didn't want. And The Sanctum has a safe word as a precaution."

"What's the safe word?" I ask.

"Red."

"So all I have to say is red if I want you to stop?" I can't imagine anything he could do that would make me want him to stop.

"That's it. We'll both walk away, no feelings hurt. No strings."

It's getting harder to process his words. My thoughts are sluggish. My blood supply having retreated to other, more pleasurable locales. "What's in it for you?"

"You," he answers, as though it's that simple.

And maybe it is.

Maybe I've been so caught up in making the right choices, doing the right thing, that I've simply forgotten to enjoy myself, my life. Even in areas like sex.

Especially areas like sex.

For so long I thought the desires I had to be taken, to be owned, were something to be ashamed of that I buried them deep down inside of me. I got tangled up in relationships like the one I just got out of in order to prove that I'm normal.

Maybe I'm not.

Maybe I'm not normal, and maybe that's okay.

"Let me give you this," he says.

Needing simplicity. Needing someone else to take charge, take the choices out of my hands for a while, I say, "Yes."

5

He guides me from the dance floor to one of the more private booths alongside the opposite wall of the main floor. There are people everywhere, the whole room is packed wall to wall with them. But the one person I want to see, the one who moves behind me, then pulls me into his lap, hasn't yet let me see his face.

When I turn to catch a glimpse, he lays his hands on my shoulders. "Not yet," he says. "This isn't about me. There will be plenty of time for that. Later." Those hands skim down my shoulders and along my arms when I don't protest.

"You aren't going to tell me who you are?"

"Not yet," he repeats.

"Then what do I call you?"

"If you need to speak you may call me sir."

"Okay," I say, already squirming in his lap, needing him and his hands. His fingers tighten on my arms in warning and I amend, "Yes, sir." Saying it here, in this setting doesn't feel as silly as I imagined it would. It feels...right.

"Did you like having them watch you?" he asks, his touch light now, his fingers dancing along my wrists. When I can't find the words to answer, one of his big palms comes to cup my neck, applying pressure there.

For a moment, I fight against being restrained, even in such a small way. My head instinctively jerks to the side, trying to break free of his hold, but he's implacable, and I don't move him an inch. His other arm winds around my waist to hold me firmly in his lap. I can't escape him, can't escape his demands, his questions, or the truth.

"Yes. Yes, sir. I liked it."

His lips ghost up the side of my neck and his hand returns beneath my skirt. "Good girl," he murmurs.

The couple from the dance floor appears, no doubt at a signal from the commanding man behind me. They sit on the plush bench to our right and continue their conversation, like I don't have a man's hands mapping my body right in front of them.

"If you get uncomfortable or want to stop, what do you say?" he asks.

The words flit around my mouth, but I can't seem to draw them out of the growing fog in my thoughts.

He drapes my thighs over his legs, spreading them in suggestion for the couple across the booth and causing my breathing to become shallow. He moves his mouth back to my ear. "What do you say?"

"R-red," I whisper back, my mouth dry.

He rewards me by putting his hands back underneath my dress. My head tips back against his shoulder as he goes right back to where he'd been on the dance floor, his fingers under my panties, except this time he adds a hand on my breast, cupping and squeezing its weight, tweaking my nipple over my dress.

I glance at the crowd milling about the rest of the floor and find the couple in our booth isn't our only audience. There are several upturned faces—not all— but a good few turned toward our display.

"Uh—"

I start to say, but he leaves my breast to put a suggestive hand over my mouth. "Remember what I said? I'll take care of you. Just enjoy it. You shouldn't feel bad for wanting the things you want. Just like I don't. You're a beautiful woman. You deserve to be wanted. You deserve their admiration."

"What do you deserve?" I say, then hastily add, "Sir."

"A beautiful woman that no one else can have but me. A woman who chose me out of a roomful of men."

His fingers are quick and efficient, undeniably talented, but I'm as interested in his words as I am in his actions. "I don't even know what you look like," I say through shuddering breaths. "I don't know anything about you."

"The only thing that matters right now is how you feel. Now be quiet. No talking until you come. We don't want to punish you on your first night here, do we?"

I open my mouth to respond and then slam it shut. The inability to talk, to worry, only leaves room for feeling. Having people watching on all sides is like being in front of a dozen different mirrors. My reactions to every carnal touch and nip and stroke is reflected on their faces, with their bright eyes and rosy cheeks.

Moans are coming from the couple in our booth now as they fondle each other. They aren't watching so much now as madly making out. I did that, I think. I made them mindless with need. My limbs tighten around his knees as my response spins wildly out of control.

"That's my good girl," he says in my ear. "They're all watching you. Wanting you. You see how much you turn them on?"

His finger slips inside me as his thumb strokes the bundle of nerves at the top of my sex. He adds another finger, stretching me wide. He's gonna take me over. Wreck me completely.

Even as I fly apart, fall to pieces, I wonder how I'm ever going to be able to come back from this.

Then, I wonder if I even want to.

My thoughts and dreams are filled with everything that happened last night as I prepare for my date with Dr. Mikhail Alexandrov. Even though I've performed on a nightly basis for years, I've never done anything on the level of what I did with the stranger at the The Sanctum. My cheeks haven't stopped burning since I returned home.

"I can't believe he cancelled on you," Mom says as she watches me put the finishing touches on my makeup.

I push thoughts from last night from my mind, certain she'll see the evidence on my face. "C'mon, you know as well as I do how hectic the E.R. can be. The last thing I want to do is make him go out on a blind date after the night he had. Besides, we both enjoy the theatre. We'll probably have a better time going to see the play than having dinner anyway."

"He's not taking you to dinner?" she says, her brows lifted.

I sigh, remembering why I left home at eighteen in the first place. "Yes, Mom. He's taking me to dinner. I'm just saying this feels more personal, like he actually asked me instead of it being a setup."

"You won't regret it. He's a good man. He—"

I cut her off. "No, don't tell me. I don't want to know anything about him so I can form my own opinions."

She smiles. "You're going to have a great time."

"I'm sure we will."

"Remember what I said about grandbabies!" Her laughter follows me out of the front door and into the balmy evening air.

A sleek, expensive looking dark SUV waits for me at the curb, right on time. Even though the windows are tinted and rolled up, I prickle with a heavy awareness. With a calming breath, I walk down the sidewalk and pull open the passenger door. Pulling it open, I take a deep breath and plaster a smile on my lips.

It takes every ounce of training I have to keep the smile fixed on my face.

Because he is gorgeous.

Make your mouth water, make your knees weak, take your breath away kind of gorgeous.

"You must be Stella," he says with a grin.

"I must be," I say as I climb into his SUV.

He holds out a friendly hand and says, "So nice to finally meet you."

"You, too."

And it is. His dark brown hair is trim and tidy, the bottom edge brushing against the top of his leather jacket. The collar of his white button-up shirt is neatly pressed and accentuates the dark line of his defined jaw.

My hormones must be on high alert because I want to kiss that space between his shirt and his jawline in the dark hollow of his throat. I study him out of the corner of my eye with a few furtive glances.

His eyes are the deep, clear blue of the Atlantic Ocean laid in striking contrast to the dark slash of his lashes and eyebrows. His lips are full, his teeth white and straight under his boyish grin. The rest of him, I notice, is all man.

He navigates through traffic with an easy confidence, his corded forearms flexing, his body angled toward me as we make polite conversation.

"You didn't have to take me to the theatre, Mikhail," I say. "I'm happy to do something else."

Shaking his head, he glances over at me. "No, this is perfect. When I moved to the U.S. my grandpa and I used to go to movies and plays to help learn the language. Some of my favorite memories are in a theatre."

"You're close with your grandpa?"

"Very. He and my grandmother moved over with my parents from Russia when I was young. We all lived in the same house until my parents could afford their own."

My own grandparents threw my mom out when she informed them she was pregnant with me and unwilling to marry my father.

"Thank you for humoring my mom. I know how pushy she can be. I promise I'll try not to be one of those horror stories you tell to your friends about, the blind date gone wrong."

He slants a heated look my way. "So far it's going absolutely right."

He makes me wait until he can jog around the front to open my door for me. I study him, wondering if he's being for real, when I step out the door. His scent wraps around me—all pine and spice—and I resist the urge to step closer into the circle of his arms to inhale it some more.

As he guides me up the steps to Will Call, my mind is a whirl of doubts, what ifs, and should I's. I gave myself one night at The Sanctum and it should be more than enough to slake my needs. Clear my mind.

But it's not.

As he urges me through the double front doors, I push The Sanctum—and the man—from my mind. This man is here, he's real, solid. Based on the butterflies fluttering like mad in my stomach, this could be the kind of man I've always dreamed of. There's no use pining for the fantasy when reality is standing right in front of me.

I didn't expect the piercing burn of longing that stabs me straight through the heart when the lights begin to dim and we take our seats in his box. Furious to find hot tears prickling my eyes, I blink rapidly and focus on studying the man next to me instead.

I didn't expect to like him either, and I don't know what to make of that.

He's the man I always imagined I'd be with. The perfect man, in fact. Steady job, polite, sense of humor, considerate. He not only paid generously for the meal beforehand, but even bought champagne and had it brought to our seats.

Sipping on the bubbly concoction, I ask, "Okay, I have to ask. How have you not been snapped up already? What? There aren't any women in the south interested in a handsome doctor?"

He glances toward the stage where the opening act begins with soft, romantic music. When he looks back, he says, "Well, one did, but we aren't together anymore."

"I'm sorry to hear that," I say.

When he doesn't say anything, I worry I overstepped an invisible line, then he wraps an arm around my shoulder, pulling me closer on the bench seats and I brush my doubts away, determined to enjoy tonight.

"You'd be great on stage," he says.

I take a sip of champagne, carefully considering my response. "Thank you. Though it's not as glamorous as it seems."

"Neither is being a doctor." He pauses for a second, taking a drink from his own glass. "Following your dreams is rarely easy."

My back stiffens and I frown. "I know."

"Do you think you'll ever go back?"

"Maybe, someday," I say after a moment. "But I'm not sure. A couple years out there with no success is hell."

"Never accept defeat," he says.

I turn to him, taking in his dark hair and blue eyes, his thoughtful expression. "I'm sorry?"

He laughs at himself. "Sorry, just something my grandpa used to say that got me through med school."

"Sounds like a smart man," I say.

"Oh he's the best. Maybe I'll take you to meet him," he glances at me with heated eyes. "Next time."

My belly tenses, butterflies revitalized. "I think I'd like that. Depending on how the rest of the night goes, of course."

He leans closer, all pine and warmth, "Upping the stakes, huh? Is this like a performance evaluation?"

"Don't worry," I say. "So far you're getting rave reviews."

For once, I'm too distracted to focus on the actors bounding across the stage in front of us. My brain is too clogged with memories of my own performances, the longing stirring a sugar-sweet ache deep in my chest. I counteract the yearning by leaning in to the white-hot heat of Mikhail's side, enjoying the comforting embrace of his strong arm wrapped around my shoulders. The ease of his touch erases some of my self-doubt.

"What are you thinking about?" he asks.

I duck my chin. "Nothing, just wondering how we end up where we do."

"Grandpa would call it luck," he says.

"Bad luck."

His fingers trace a pattern on my arm as he watches the play and considers his response. "Well, didn't you say the other day you have to take the good with the bad?"

Laughing, I say, "Already turning my own words against me."

We watch the remainder of the play in silence, but it's a comfortable one. A silence fraught with pulses of elation as his fingers secretly map the overly sensitized flesh on the inside of my arm. Our legs brush once, twice, and stay pressed together, hip to hip, when they meet the third time.

When it ends and people start filing out, he holds me in the protective, possessive, curve of his arm and I let him.

Anticipation rises as he leads me to his car. I'd been kidding about giving him a performance evaluation, but the closer we get to my mom's house the more I imagine the good night kiss. It's ridiculous how my fingers tremble and I have to hold them steady in my lap. Ridiculous that after what I did last night, the thoughts I still have, that something as simple as a kiss can make my knees loose and watery.

He pulls to a stop in front of my mom's house and my breath freezes in my chest. We share a heated glance before he smiles and hops out to open my door again. I try to ignore the flutter in my stomach, try to catch my breath, but the effort is wasted as soon as he reaches my side.

This time, he doesn't give me room to move by him, instead he pulls me out into his arms and my breath comes out in a whoosh. His gaze meets mine with bold assurance. There's no teasing glint in his eyes now. He's a man sure of what he wants and what he wants...is me.

Then he says in a voice like the low purr of a well-satisfied feline, "Just to give you something to think about," right before he lowers his head to press his soft, warm lips against mine.

Desire, banked by uncertainty and nerves, roars to life between us. The kiss itself doesn't catch me off guard. Based on the looks and touches he's been giving me all night, he's been waiting to do just this. What surprises me is the barely restrained lust I feel thrumming underneath his own skin. I can feel it in the way he keeps the kiss the barest press of lips, how he keeps a slight distance between our bodies, even as his chest and thighs brush against my own.

In that restraint, my body roars to life. My previously hesitant hands release their hold on my purse, letting it drop to the floorboard with a muffled thump. They wrap around the supple leather of his collar to hold him to me. I'm tall for a woman, but he is so much taller. Even in heels, I have to lift on the balls of my feet to fit close to him.

Beneath my questing hands, his body is as hard and unyielding as granite. His own hands grip my waist with the same possessive, persistent grip he used to guide me all night. It's the perfect contrast to the man from The Sanctum. Where he'd made me feel dangerous and sexy, Misha makes me feel delicate and feminine. I sigh into his mouth, leaning into his chest and tipping my head back.

And it's as if that is the signal he's been waiting for because the kiss turns hungry and carnal. It deepens, appetite whetted by the barest brush of lips and teeth and tongue. He explores my mouth, drugging me with his scent and taste, as if testing to see how long and how far I'll let him take the kiss.

Need, temporarily slaked by my risqué adventures from the night before, burns hot and bright behind my closed lids. It coats my sensible lingerie between my legs and perfumes the air around us.

Pressed against him, a thought streaks though my head as electrifying as lighting itself.

I'm so screwed.

6

I shouldn't want him. Shouldn't want the things he does to me.

But I do.

I should turn around, go back to the safety and security of a man like Mikhail, but I can't stop thinking about the man from The Sanctum, how he made me feel. I want it again, have to have it again.

Just one more time.

Or at least, that's what I tell myself as I pull into the secluded parking lot located underneath The Sanctum's nondescript structure. After my last visit, I was accepted for membership, having been approved by the owners. Today, I'll be put into the system, a full fledged member rather than a guest.

In the days since I was here last, I'd done a lot of research. Learned most clubs like this meant what they touted about the privacy of their clients. For which I am grateful. My mom may be a free bird, but I sure as hell don't want to hear what she'll have to say if she finds out I returned home from New York to join a BDSM club.

Despite that, I've never felt as at home anywhere else, except on stage. Walking into the club, aside from the initial nervousness, was like finding a piece of myself I hadn't known I lost. I don't know if it's going to be as easy to let this newfound freedom go when the time comes.

And it will. I've already made another date with Mikhail. Maybe the two sides of my life, the two sides of me, will never even have to meet.

My knees are wobbling, tense with anticipation as I trek across the garage to the member's only entrance. Then I hear it. Somehow I know it's him. The hairs on the back of my neck prickle and my skin starts tingling. The low purr of his engine comes to a stop behind me in the parking spot nearest to the entrance.

Knowing his penchant for privacy and secrecy, I don't give in to the temptation to turn around and catch a glimpse of his face, even though I want nothing more. I feel his weighted gaze on me, already enticing my submission, my confession, my pleas. He hasn't even touched me yet, and I'm wet for him.

Suddenly, feeling him watch me has my chest growing too tight for my short inhalations. My exposed skin prickles, coming to attention, knowing he's near and aching for the commanding touch of his hands. A breeze caresses the dips behind my knees, the hollow of my throat, and my temples where perspiration has collected.

His boots echo in the empty parking garage, then come to a stop just behind me. I imagine I can very nearly feel his heat, even as the night air whisks it away.

"Head to the third floor. Group Room number 4 is reserved for our scene tonight. Whenever you join me here you'll put your things in the lockers, go to the room and undress. Then put on the blindfold on the table and kneel by the door and wait for me. Do you understand?"

"Yes, sir," I say.

I do as he asks, rushing up the three flights of stairs in a flash. The dark hallways are deserted and even though I'm sure the rooms are sound-proofed I imagine all sorts of erotic scenes taking place behind the closed doors. There are a few women in the women's locker rooms, but I keep my head down as I take one of the empty lockers to store my things.

The doors to the owner's suites and business offices are pulled shut as well as those for a couple other private rooms and the Fisse Prive—I'd googled the name when I got a tour of The Sanctum online and realized it is the spanking room. The thought makes me shiver as I walk the short hallway down, across from the Fisse Prive to the group room. My name is on the reservation for this slot and I know that must be intentional. I give a passing thought to his identity before the growing urgency in my blood pushes me over the threshold and into the shadowed room.

It takes seconds for me to strip to the practical, but still sexy, black panties. I fold my clothes and place them on an unobtrusive chair in the corner by the door, then I settle on my knees with the blindfold over my eyes.

Seconds, minutes, hours pass with sluggish intensity. Sweat returns to all the valleys and dips along my curves as I wait. I perch on my haunches, knees spread, bare chest thrust out and ready, waiting for his attention.

My heart nearly pounds its way out of my chest when I hear the door open and close. He doesn't come right to me, and it takes a few moments for me to piece together that he's doing it on purpose. Wanting to keep me waiting, needy, and on tenterhooks.

Metal snaps together. Footsteps click against the floor. I try to keep my head slanted toward the ground, but each taste of sound is a mystery I want to solve and ears tilt this way and that to try and discern what he has planned.

Finally, I detect his slow, steady steps coming to where I kneel waiting.

My fingers clutch desperately against my thighs, my nails digging into the skin. A hand, steady and sure, cups my chin and he leans down to press a firm, unflinching kiss on my ready lips. He rubs back and forth, more to tease than satiate.

"Is my good girl ready?" he asks, his fingers caressing my lips, still sensitive from his kiss. "You look so sweet for me on your knees like this."

Sensing it's a rhetorical question, I bite my tongue to keep from begging for him to touch me.

His hand coasts from my lips, up and over my cheek, and dives into my hair. Then tightens, stinging my scalp with a pleasure-pain that shoots straight to the place throbbing and sensitive between my legs. He cups the back of my head and guides me to my feet and slowly across the room. The wood floors are cold and hard underneath my bare feet. He stops me after a bit and his hands position me facing opposite him.

I hear chains rustling and my abs tighten, my imagination running wild, wondering what he's going to do.

"This room is intended for large group scenes," he says. "I've modified it a little today so everyone can watch what I'm doing to you if they want to. You can't see it but in front of you is a wall of two way mirrors and on the other side, I imagine there's quite the growing crowd."

My thighs clench together.

"You like that? You like everyone watching you be a good little slut?" he asks as he wraps a piece of something—leather, or maybe thick cloth?—around my wrists. He attaches them to the length of chain, and I realize it's a pulley. He's going to string me up for everyone to see as he does whatever he likes to me. My ragged breathing is his only answer. Even if he let me speak, I don't think my mouth could form the words.

The darkness is complete, absolute, all-encompassing—and I relish it nearly as much as I relished the weighted feel of his gaze on my bared flesh.

The pulley inches upwards, stretching my arms to full extension above my head. Not so much that it became painful, or overly so, but just enough to spear awareness through my joints and birth a pleasurable warmth in my quivering muscles. I knew the spectacle I must make, splayed naked in the middle of a dark room like a feast...or an offering.

I want to be both; I will be both. At least, once more. A taste to satiate the growing desires inside me. A farewell to the parts of me I don't quite understand. They've always been there, just beneath the surface. And he's determined to discover each and every one of them.

"You're going to be so good for me aren't you," he says from somewhere close. The parts of the room I had been able to make out before the blindfold were all black. A single black table covered with implements, floggers of all sizes, straps and belts to fasten a body to any of the various setups in the room, and a black bag —the contents of which I can only imagine. And my imagination is vivid. The walls are draped with thick black curtains. It muffles his movements, making it hard for me to discern his location and heightening my awareness. "What a pretty picture you make."

Even though my eyes are covered, I lower them. My pleasure, my pain, is his. I'm his. If others are watching through the two way windows, they're at the back of my mind. His attention is far more exhilarating than a hundred pairs of eyes.

"What do you want me to do to you?"

I take a deep breath. Exhale. *Anything.* "Everything."

"Is there anything you'd prefer I didn't use?"

A shiver courses through me, imagining what he'll choose. The anticipation is almost as sweet as the action. "No," I answer once I catch my breath.

"Anything off limits?" His voice is closer now, and I imagine I can feel his breath on my skin.

"I want you to do what makes you happy. I trust you."

My sense of hearing overcompensates for my loss of sight and I hear the catch in his throat, before he says, "Are you certain that's wise? This is your first time doing a scene like this."

"With you, yes. I wouldn't be here if I didn't. That's the whole point isn't it? To trust you." By this point I'm shaking, but not just from the sweet pain from my extended arms. My body calls to him, for his touch, for his cock. I want anything and everything he has to give and more.

"You'll let me decide what the point is tonight," he murmurs from behind me, his heated breath coasting over my bare skin like a caress. I test the length of the restraints, arching back, scooting on my toes to try and make contact with the firm expanse of his chest, needing to touch him, almost as much as I need what comes next.

Cool air wraps around me as he retreats. "Did I say you could move?"

My pussy clenches at the steel threading through his voice. *Yes. This is it.*

I tuck my chin farther into my chest. "No."

"No, what?" he bites out, slapping a palm against my naked ass.

"No, sir," I amend. A fine sheen of sweat coats my skin and tremors dance beneath.

His voice is a deep rumble in his chest. "I think you need a reminder. Already. Maybe you're looking for punishment."

I tuck my fingers around the material extending from my bound wrists for extra grip. Metal scrapes against wood, followed by soft, measured footsteps. Heat touches my foot, the firm grip of his tapered fingers. He positions a thick band around the top of my foot and buckles it down to one of the latches fixed on the floor. After he does the same to the other, he checks to make sure neither are too tight and when he's done, I'm well and truly at his mercy, unable to move.

He pats my thigh and says, "Tell me if you experience any discomfort or strain." When I don't answer he gives my ass a little slap, and I say, "Yes, sir."

I hear him walk away again and retrieve something from the table, my mind goes wild imagining what it can be, how the people on the other side are reacting, but more than anything, it's the not knowing that causes perspiration to build and my muscles to quiver.

His warmth reaches my back first, then his arms wrap around my waist. A thin cloth belt wraps around my hips and they jerk back a little at the contact, brushing against his jeans-clad legs. He situates the belt around and between my legs, buckling it on the side when it fits to his satisfaction. Then he clicks a smooth piece to the front, and my stomach drops. The slim bullet fits into a pocket in the crotch of the panties and presses intimately against my sex.

Tossing my head back, I almost wish I had a gag to swallow my responses. He's barely started, and I already want to scream out my frustration.

"Shh," he whispers against the shell of my ear. "We're just getting started."

There's a click and a buzzing fills the air. I jerk, trying to get away from the unrelenting pressure, but with my legs and arms restrained and barely any give in the line, there's nowhere for me to hide.

Which is, no doubt, exactly what he has in mind.

A hand wraps around my throat, arching my back against his chest. His voice is a gentle threat above the hum of vibrations. "If you come before I say so, it'll be the only time you come tonight. Understand?"

That's an impossibility.

Already, the first sparks of an orgasm bloom low in my abdomen. My legs are shaking with the effort to hide from the non-stop stimulation, but no matter how far I strain, I can't get away. I'm so distracted by the sensations and concentration on not coming, that when a whoosh splits the air and a stinging slices across the cheeks of my ass, a scream tears from my throat.

It's a never-ending cycle of pleasure and pain.

He releases a stream of alternating soft and hard strikes, first across the meat of my ass and then at the crease where my ass meets my legs. The shock sends me arching into the vibrating bullet and then the cycle starts all over again.

The rising crescendo of pleasure is punctuated by his gruff commands and the ever looming threat of the audience watching just on the other side of the glass wall. I hover on the edge for an interminable amount of time, struggling to obey his command, but wanting to give in, wanting to give in so bad, tears leak from the corners of my eyes.

His hands soothe, even as the flogger's sting turns my backside nearly numb. He alternates directions, amount of pressure, massaging away the bite only to strike again just when sensation returns.

I hear a thud, then feel the flogger roll to a stop by my bare feet. By now, I've given up trying to control my breathing, my sobs, and my chest is heaving, stomach contracting. His hands dance along my backside, then climb up my ribs and up to cup and lift my bared breasts. He scissors my nipples between his fingers, tweaking and tugging until I'm mindless with it. I hear a woman sobbing and it gives me pause until I realize the woman....is me.

"Please, please, please, sir. Can I come? I need to come."

He tweaks my nipples again, and I'm afraid I nearly come undone. I hover there on the precipice until he nibbles my shoulder and says, ever so softly, "Yes, give it to me."

"When can I see you again?" he asks.

The audience is gone, no doubt having left after a subtle signal from my companion as I was coming down from my orgasm-induced high. He immediately clicked off the bullet and carefully released my feet and arms from the restraints. Now he holds me in his arms, still blindfolded, as he gives me a thorough rubdown that's as much to return circulation to my limbs as it is to ground me.

"I don't know," I say carefully. "I've got some things going on in my personal life and I'm not sure if it will leave much time for me in the next few weeks."

"Shame," he murmurs.

Leaning against his firm chest with drowsiness creeping around the edges, I yawn, feeling warm, and safe, and right at home. "What's a shame?" I slur.

"I haven't been to The Sanctum in a long time. It's just a shame we won't get to spend more time together. Unless I'm mistaken and you didn't enjoy tonight."

"No, I did," I rush to correct him. "Very much. In case you didn't notice."

He chuckles, and I snuggle closer to his warmth as his hand caresses the length of my spine. "No, I did," he assures me. "Your face was a sight everyone will be talking about for weeks. They'll no doubt be sad to hear there won't be a repeat performance for some time."

Doubt creeps into the haze of the afterglow and I sit up, the air suddenly stifling. "I'm not ruling it out. This is just new for me."

He brushes a hand over my hair, presses a kiss to

my temple. "I know. No strings remember? Now lay here on this bench for a few minutes and let me tend to you. Then, I'll let you go."

As he rubs me down with a soothing cooling gel and tends to my tender ass and legs, I know I'm going to have to think long and hard about whether or not *I* want to let *him* go.

But not just him.

I'll have to think long and hard about whether or not I'm going to let this newfound side of me go, too.

7

H

e leaves first, closing the door silently behind him.

After a few seconds, when I'm sure he's gone, I pull down the blindfold and heave deep breaths. Aftershocks are long gone, but my sensitized skin still prickles with awareness. At some point, he must have dressed me in a robe, because it's warm softness is quite possibly the most comfortable thing I've ever worn.

I'm almost tempted to take it home with me as I pad down the empty hallway back to the lockers. With a look of regret, I stuff it in the laundry bin full of identical robes and redress in my regular clothes. My limbs are still trembling as I tug on my shoes and shoulder my purse.

By the time I get back down to the parking garage, I manage to regain control over myself—for the most part. My muscles are languid and my breathing now slow and steady. I practically pour myself into the front seat of my car.

Out of habit, I check my phone, hoping to see a callback from one of the art programs I applied to at nearby colleges and troupes, with no luck. There is, however, a text from Mikhail.

> Mikhail: I'm afraid this is becoming a habit, but I'll have to cancel on the date with my grandpa. He passed away this morning.

All good feelings from my session drain away. I'd been looking forward to meeting him, seeing them together. The way Mikhail talks about him, the way his face looked when he described his childhood, I knew they had a close relationship.

> Me: Is there anything I can do? Do you need anything?

I don't know what else to say. I've always been extremely awkward when people experience loss, having never really experienced any of my own. It's always just been my mother and I against the world.

When I pull up to my mom's house, my phone buzzes in my lap. I glance at the text as I unfold from the car and head inside.

> Mikhail: No, but thank you. I'm sorry to bail for a second time, but I have to meet with the funeral home to make arrangements.

Heart aching, I call, because this isn't something he should have to do over text.

He answers and it almost brings tears to my own eyes when his voice comes over the line, thick with emotion, "Hello?"

"You don't need to apologize, Mikhail," I say.

Clearing his throat, he says, "I think you can call me Misha now."

"Misha," I say softly. "There is nothing for you to apologize for. Are you sure there's nothing I can do? I can put together a mean casserole or something."

"Thank you, that's very kind. I've got a meeting with him in about an hour and after that I—" he pauses for a second, then says, "You know what? I would like for you to do something with me tonight, after. If you don't already have something planned."

I kick off my shoes as I enter the living room. "Anything. Name it."

"My grandpa always had a tattoo of a pin up girl—something he got when he joined the military after he immigrated to the U.S. I always thought I'd get one when he passed. Just to remember him. Would you go with me? Kind of an odd request, but I'd rather not be alone tonight. If you can't, it's—"

Hearing the aching loss reflected in his voice, I blurt, "Of course I will."

"Thanks for coming," Mikhail—Misha—says as he opens the door for me to get out of his car. A bright storefront is in front of us with the parlors name emblazoned in neon. The drive over was quiet, both of us lost to our own thoughts.

"Of course. I've always wanted to go to a tattoo parlor and anything to take your mind off of it."

He takes my hand as he leads me over puddles of murky water. "I'm pretty sure your smile took care of most of it." I squeeze his hand and follow him inside.

The smell hits me as soon as we cross the threshold—cleaning products, air freshener, and a metallic tang that I also taste in the back of my throat. It's also ridiculously cold, the huge A/C unit in the back, furiously pumping cold air. To our right is a glass counter piled high with various three-ringed binders. Inside the display cases are a multitude of piercing accessories and after-care products.

Misha greets the man behind the counter, a scruffy beast of a guy with colorful ink on both of his arms and a full beard, though his head is completely shaved. "Jake, good to see you."

"Misha, man. I'd like to say it's good to see you, except I know why you're here." Jake grabs Misha's hand and pulls him into a one-armed, back-slapping hug. "You ready?"

"As I'll ever be." Misha grabs my hand. "Jake, this is my friend Stella. Stella, this is Jake. He'll be torturing me today."

I give Jake an easy smile. "Nice to meet you."

"Glad you could come with our boy here," Jake says. "I guess we'll see how he does under the gun."

Nodding and looking around at the artwork on the walls, I say, "You've got a nice place here. I may have to come back."

"You got any ink?" Jake asks as he leads us back to his immaculate station.

"No, not yet. I've always been interested, though. Just haven't found anything that speaks to me yet."

"Misha, take a seat right here, buddy." Jake wiggles

his eyebrows. "You'll have to lose the shirt for me, though."

That makes Misha smile, and any reservations I had about bringing him here when he's so obviously hurting wash away. Maybe taking ink into his body, memorializing his grandfather's memory permanently, is his way of carrying that memory on with him forever.

Misha crosses his arms in front of his chest and peels off his shirt. My mouth goes dry and I nearly miss the chair I'm aiming for and fall ass first onto the sparkling white linoleum. Thankfully, I only fumble a bit and manage to sit without looking like a total idiot.

I shouldn't be staring at his bare chest when he's mourning this way. I absolutely shouldn't. When a quick glance turns into ogling, I force myself to pull away and study what Jake is doing—anything to take my mind off his powerful shoulders and tapered abdomen.

He gathers up what looks like little paint caps full of brilliant color, a tattoo gun, sterilizing materials and paper towels. Around us, a couple other artists are working on other people at their stations. The atmosphere pulses with music blasting from an ancient boom box and the chatter as people try to yell over the volume.

"How did you meet Misha?" I ask as he buzzes the tattoo gun a couple times, then sets it on his stainless steel tray. They share a look, and I realize that must be a personal topic. "I'm sorry," I say. "I'm just making conversation. Totally looks like I put my foot in my mouth."

"No," Misha says, putting a warm hand on my knee. "Not at all."

"Not a secret," Jake adds. "Misha here was my daughters doctor."

"Oh," I say. "What happened?"

Jake takes an outline of the tattoo and applies it on Misha's shoulder. He holds it there while he finishes the story. "She was six when she got into an accident, semi driver fell asleep at the wheel and slammed into her mother's car when they were coming home from a friend's birthday party. Misha was working the ER when she came in."

I'm almost afraid to hear the end.

"She didn't make it," Jake says gently, and I realize, stunned, that his soft tone is more to comfort me than himself. "Misha, though. He didn't give up for hours. He worked on her until the end. He never gave up. I told him, when I was able to think straight enough, that his first tattoo was on me." Jake shrugs out of his button up shirt to show me a shockingly realistic portrait of his daughter.

"He pestered me until I agreed," Misha corrects.

Jake waves that away as he changes into a fresh pair of gloves. "Now I can pay him back for everything he did for my girl."

Misha keeps his eyes on his lap, but not before I see the sorrow painting his face. I don't say anything, but I take his hand in my own as Jake goes to work on his tattoo. We don't talk much as Jake works, aside from me asking questions about what Jake's doing or Misha griping to bust Jake's balls.

But the connection is there. Real.

Because he doesn't let go of my hand the whole time.

8

By the time I get back to Mom's house, it's nearly midnight and I can barely see straight. It takes three tries before I'm able to fit my key into the lock, and even then I have to focus to put one foot in front of the other to get over the threshold. The place in my chest where my heart is supposed to be is numb from overwork, from bleeding for Misha, from being torn in two directions.

I know what it's like to be without a father figure. To wonder and worry and be hyperaware of the empty place at the dinner table, at soccer games and graduations. If I'd actually known my father and lost him after having a full life of those memories, that emptiness would be unbearable.

Closing the door behind me, I face plant into the comfy sofa, hoping to wring some small amount of comfort from it's familiar surface. Exhaustion turns my vision gray and just as I'm starting to eek off into slumber, a sound pulls me from the edge of unconsciousness.

My ears strain and it comes again.

A giggle.

From my mom's room.

I press my face into the couch cushions. Dear God, please no.

She giggles again, followed by the low tones of a man's voice.

Jesus Christ she has to be nearing fifty, how is she still going strong?

And how in the hell am I supposed to sneak back to my room without alerting the happy couple? Do I even want to spend the rest of the night sharing a bedroom wall with them?

Coming home was supposed to be the easy part.

Maybe the couch is a better choice.

Mom's squeal carries down the hallway.

Yep, a much better choice.

I'm just drifting over the edge when her door opens. Wincing into the pillows, I try to feign sleep.

Her tiptoes inch down the hallway and toward the kitchen. They pause in the entryway.

Then, "Stella?"

I swallow the groan, but she's always been able to read me.

"Stella, I know you're awake. What are you doing on the couch? I thought you were staying with Dr. Alexandrov?"

Kissing my sweet dreams goodbye, I sit up, wiping the sleep from my eyes. "It wasn't that kind of date, Mom."

I can see her twinkling eyes all the way across the room. She glances back at her room and then at me. "Honey, it's always that kind of date."

She chuckles all the way into the kitchen, and I follow her because I'm already up and my stomach is making the lack of dinner known. "What do you mean?"

Flashing me a puzzled frown, she says, "You lived in New York. I'm sure you dated around. I thought for sure Dr. A was going to be your type."

Settling at the little dinette with an orange and a cup of tea, I say, "I didn't say he isn't my type."

Mom grins impishly. "See! I knew it!"

I roll my eyes. "His grandpa just died. It's not exactly the time to jump anyone's bones."

"You're too serious, sometimes, Stel. That's why I wanted to hook the both of you up. After his—" she cuts herself off, her eyes wide. "I'm just saying."

Licking the juice off my fingers, I study her. "Yes. What were you saying?"

"Nothing sweetheart. I'm just happy you found someone you get along with," she answers a little too brightly. "I better get back."

She kisses me on the brow and saunters down the hallway to a welcoming cat call from her gentlemen friend.

The next evening, after a hard night's sleep I spend the after lunch hours submitting applications to a couple of other prospective jobs and internships—none of which seem like they'll bear any fruit, but they're worth the effort. Especially a grad program at a neighboring college. One that has connections to people in the theatre world.

Pretty much the type of thing I'd kill for right now, especially since I can't imagine doing anything other than being on stage.

I haven't gotten any texts from the man I've been

meeting at The Sanctum and I don't know whether or not I'm grateful. For a moment, I'm glad I don't have to push the issue. A time will come when I have to pick between Misha, the man I'm quickly falling for, and the man who seems to know every inch of my body better than I do.

As I'm leaving a café with a cappuccino and a scone after my job hunt, I do, however, get a text from Misha inviting me to his office for his lunch break. Apparently, not even a death in the family will keep the man from going into work.

Knowing he has no other relatives and knowing he probably won't accept the sympathy from anyone else, I get in my bucket of rust and head to the hospital. Of course, I forget that my mom is also working the evening shift, so color us both stunned when I run smack into her in the emergency room hallway.

"Stella. How nice of you to come by and see me at work! Why didn't you say you were coming? I could have given you a ride."

"Uh, hi, mom!"

"Hi, sweetie." Her brows furrow. She pauses and says, "What are you doing here?"

"Um, I came to see you!" I improvise.

"You just saw me last night...and this morning." Realization dawns, her brows now up near her hairline. "Ohmygoodness. You're here to see Dr. A, aren't you?" Her squeal draws the eyes of every patient in the waiting room. At my scowl, she drags me around the corner and out of their view. "He's just in his office. Go around the corner, then the first office on the left. His name is on the door there. You can't miss it. Make sure he doesn't stay here too long, okay? He'd work himself to the bone if we didn't kick him out every now and again."

"I'll try. See you later."

"Go get 'em, tiger," she says, grinning wildly. I roll my eyes at her again and give her a little wave.

I find him as I round the corner to his office. He's standing just in front of me talking to a pair of nurses.

God, he's attractive. Even more so in his lab coat and slacks, his stethoscope knotted in one pocket. Even though his eyes are drawn and somewhat lifeless and his smile doesn't quite reach them, he's still, quite possibly, the best-looking man I've ever seen. All competence and hollow cheeks. I have the sudden urge to muss him up a little, untuck his proper shirt and run my hands through his perfect hair.

Then he finishes his business with the nurses and turns to find me standing just by the corner. His smile brightens, transforming his face. "*Stellichka.*"

I don't know what it means, but the light Russian

accent he lets come through stirs my butterflies back to life. "Hi."

"You didn't have to drop everything to come," he says, crossing the hall and enveloping me in his arms. I breathe him in and squeeze him tight.

"Of course I did." I pull back and look up to his face, wishing I was a doctor so I could take away some of his pain. "No one should be alone after they lose someone."

His eyes cloud over, but he covers it so quickly, I'm not sure I even saw it in the first place. "Come sit with me in my office. I've got some paperwork to finish and then maybe we can grab a bite to eat?"

"Sounds good to me. What are you even doing at work today?" I ask as he draws me in the room.

"I'm a workaholic," he says with an easy smile.

"How's the tattoo?" I ask.

He flexes his shoulder. "Sore as hell, but worth it. Thank you for going with me, for coming here."

"Of course, whatever you need." I say as I take a chair opposite his executive style desk.

"What do you feel like having?" he asks as he shuffles through some papers.

"Whatever you want."

He gives me a little smirk. "You aren't one of those women, are you?"

Not sure if I should feel affronted, I say, "What kind of woman is that?"

"The kind who can't make up her mind about what we're going to eat so we argue about it for the next ten minutes until you tell me what it is you want."

He's smiling. God, it's a big, beautiful smile that brings out the slightest lines at the corners of his pretty blue eyes. Wanting to keep him smiling, I say, "I'm serious. We can have whatever you want."

Those pretty blue eyes heat and for a second I feel exactly like a rabbit pinned by a sleek, sly fox. There's something feral around the edge of his lips and the intensity of his gaze.

If the man from The Sanctum commands me with words and punishment, Misha can do so with his eyes alone.

After margaritas and fresh, spicy tacos, Misha invites me to his house. A little tipsy and more than a lot into him, I agree.

He does the opening my door thing again, something I'm not sure if I'll ever get used to, and takes my hand. Something else I'm not sure I'll get used to. I never thought I'd be the type of woman to enjoy constant, casual affection. A brush of his hand on the small of my back as he leads me to the restaurant. A finger on my lip to wipe away a bit of picante sauce. His hand hot and hard on my thigh. He doles it out like second nature, and I find myself greedy for it. Like a flower gone too long without sun.

It's not until we're coming up the walk that I actually look up and take in his house. The sweeping porch, exposed beams and farmhouse charm is definitely not what I was expecting.

"My parents left it and the farm to me in their will. I could never quite make myself sell it. Grandpa liked to come over sometimes and remember them. And it's a great neighborhood, if I ever decided to have a family."

"It's wonderful. And so big!" I look around in awe. "I think it's bigger than my whole floor in New York."

He laughs as he opens the door for me to walk in. "I like my space."

The interior is light and bright, even though the sun is already setting. The walls are a beautiful exposed white shiplap that's common in the south and are accented with antiques and soft blues and greens. The whole space is open from entryway to kitchen. I can even see an expansive backyard through the

French doors on the far side of the eat-in nook. "I'll say."

As he steps in and takes off his coat and tie, hanging them on the hooks by the door, I study the pictures on the walls. I find one of him when he was young, surrounded by his parents and his grandpa. They look happy. What I imagine a real family looks like.

A pang echoes in my chest and when I look at the next picture, recognizing Misha next to a beautiful blonde bombshell, the pang nearly steals my breath away.

"Is this your ex-wife?" I ask, hating the insecurity that makes my voice thin. "She's beautiful."

He turns me away from the picture, his hands cupping my cheeks so I have to look into his eyes. "You're beautiful, *Stellichka*," he says with such conviction, I forget my moment of petty jealousy.

I twine my arms around his neck and pull his mouth down to mine. His hands skim down my rumpled tunic dress and grip the bare skin of my thighs. My knees buckle when he grips the spot just beneath my ass to press me against him. I lift my hands to his chest for balance, clutching the collar of his button-up shirt.

His big hands lift me up and he leverages his weight to press me against the wall next to the panoramic, floor-to-ceiling windows in his living room. I try not to think about his neighbors, about how they may happen by a window and look into his and see us. They aren't terribly close, but close enough to send my senses into hyperawareness. My heart thuds a quick tattoo in my ribs and I moan into his mouth, spurring his hands to wander up and underneath the hem of my dress.

Reaching down, I try to stop them, try to pull away and protest. We should go to his bedroom. Find a bed, like a normal couple, somewhere not out in the open like this, where anyone can see. The thought nearly makes me laugh, but the wave of an orgasm is already swelling inside of me just from the threat of an audience. He quells my protest with a nip of his teeth. My hands change direction, aiming his closer to the need pulsing between my legs.

I see a light flick on out of the corner of my eye and my head drops back against the wall. Misha's lips trace my jaw and the line of my throat with deft precision. His hands are urging my hips in a subtle rhythm against his thigh and I want to wrap my body around him like ivy around a pole.

"Let's go upstairs," I say into the shadows.

"No," he says, following the line of my shirt to my exposed cleavage. "Right here. Now."

"But," I murmur, the word breaking off in the middle on a strangled moan. "The windows."

He chuckles as he pulls down my shirt to bare my breasts. "No one's watching," he says.

"You don't know that," I say.

"You're right." I nearly choke and then he adds, "I'm watching. I want to watch you. I want to watch you come all over my fingers, then I'll watch you come while I use my mouth on you, then again all over my cock."

With a desperate sound, I pull him closer, needing to taste him again. His purely masculine taste and the tang from the margarita is intoxicating, intensifying my lightheadedness. His nimble fingers slip under my dress and pull my panties to the side. My breath catches and our eyes meet and my arms tighten around his shoulders. He doesn't break eye contact and for one guilty moment, I imagine the man from The Sanctum is him. As he works me up, up, up, I look at him and wish he was. As I fly over the first peak, I imagine them both watching me lose control, then I forget everything but him.

My legs are shaking by the time I come down. Disoriented, it takes me a moment to realize Misha's already on his knees. With a devilish grin, he drapes one of my legs over his shoulders. I don't have time to think, or catch my breath—which is most certainly his plan, and it's diabolical—before his tongue turns my knees to water with it's precision. Incredibly, he brings me to the edge again, but this time he holds me there. One hand keeping my leg clamped to his shoulder and the other holds my dress up so he can watch the effects of his ministrations play across my face.

I grip his head with both hands, wanting both to ease his unrelenting assault and make sure it never ends. He adjusts his shoulders to cup my hips with both hands to bring me ever closer to the careful flicks of his tongue.

Another light flicks on next door, drawing my attention to the wide open windows with a jerk of my neck. Cool air rushes across my heated cheeks. Shadows move behind the curtains. There are people there. My thighs tighten in his hold and I try to wiggle my hips back, but his grip is immovable. Caught, pinned, forced to feel everything, my breath stops up in my throat and I let out a silent scream as I fly out into the night's sky.

When he drapes me over the couch and arranges my legs over his shoulders and takes me over again, I forget about The Sanctum. I forget about the man. I forget about my own lack of direction and my worries and my future.

The only thing I think about is him as he brings me up and over again.

And again.

And again.

9

"**S**tay with me, *Stellichka*," Misha says as he reclines, unabashedly naked in his bed. The early dawn light is buttery over his sinful Egyptian cotton sheets. He looks good enough to eat and he knows it, if his grin is any indication.

"I'll come back. I just have something I need to do and then I'll come back, I promise." I glance at him as I search for my bra and panties in the wreckage from our long, long night sex-fest. Aha! I find my bra on top of his dresser and my panties hanging from his bathroom door.

"Come here," he says, sitting up against his reclaimed wood headboard. "One kiss and I'll let you go."

Slipping into my panties and wincing at the soreness of my thighs and back, I shake my head. "Oh no, we've played that game. One kiss could mean anything."

"On the lips," he says. I give him a look as I clasp my bra and hunt down my dress. "Dirty girl," he very nearly growls. "Fine, one kiss on your *mouth* and I'll let you go."

I drag on my tunic dress and come to stand next to the bed. "One kiss."

He smiles, tucking his hands behind his back. "I won't even touch you," he says.

I narrow my eyes, but put one knee on the bed, bracing my hands on his strong shoulders, careful to keep the tips of my fingers away from the tender skin near his tattoo. As I lean closer, I'm relieved to find his face is smooth, unworried, and his smile is easy. Closing my eyes, I press my lips to his.

Even without touching me, I feel his kiss down to my bones, warming me from the inside out, causing a flush to break out on my skin. He slumps down and gravity forces me to follow, brushing our chests together. Momentum has me throwing a leg over his hips to break my fall, aligning us center to center.

Heat against heat.

His hardness, against my softness.

I pull away, eyes narrowed.

"What?" he asks, feigning innocence. "I didn't touch you."

Weekdays at The Sanctum are an altogether different affair than the weekend. The main floor is no longer the hedonistic haven it was the night I met him. Now, it looks like every other restaurant in Nassau. Unremarkable, ordinary.

Interesting how all the decadent things have a veneer of sophistication and normality in the daylight.

Knowing he'll find me, somehow he always does, I wander across the first floor to the members' entrance that leads to the second. I press my thumb into the scanner and open the door after it beeps.

The race up to the third floor is a quick one, fueled by an aching want and humming anticipation. The room he's reserved for our last session is unoccupied. Following his instructions, I locate the customary blindfold and slip it over my eyes. I kneel beside the door and wait for him to enter.

He keeps me waiting this time. Maybe he already knows I'm wavering. Can he sense my interest in another man? Knowing him, knowing how much he understands *me*, he must. Even in the short amount of time we've spent together, he can read me, read my body, like no one I've ever known.

Emotion clogs my throat and I breathe deeply through my nose to stave off the tears.

How am I ever supposed to let go of this side of me?

How am I supposed to choose?

The door opens before I'm able to sort through my feelings. I can sense him by the entrance, a coil of potential energy.

"Are you purposefully tempting me to punish you, girl?" he asks when he sees I haven't changed out of my street clothes.

I don't know. Maybe I am. So I say nothing.

He crosses the room and fists a hand in my hair, pulling me to my knees. His breath is ragged, like he was so anxious he took the stairs two at a time to get to me. My stomach twists.

"Have you been a bad girl?" he asks, his voice low. When I don't answer he sucks a breath through his teeth. "You'll answer me," he says.

Silence stretches between us, it burns my cheeks and brings tears to my eyes. I want to answer him. I want to tell him...what, I don't know, but I can't seem to make the words come out of my mouth.

He releases my hair, and I stumble back like a boat without an anchor. His footsteps cross the room and he's nearly to the door before I come to my senses.

I rip off the blindfold, blinking to acclimatize to the ambient light. His dark form is nearly through the door before I catch up to him. I reach out, grabbing his shoulder and he hisses, ducking a little to remove my hand.

Even when he turns, my brain can't quite process what it's seeing.

Can't wrap around the fact that my two worlds are colliding.

Then he takes a step towards me and says, "*Stellichka.*"

I pause, but only for a second. Then relief, despite the deception, bursts through me and I smile.

Without further hesitation, I move toward him.

Epilogue

Mikhail

I run a hand through my hair, then roll my eyes at my reflection in the rearview mirror. After eleven hours on shift, where the decisions I make could result in life or death, it's opening the door and meeting a woman that has my hands damn near trembling. Gritting my teeth, I palm my phone and keys, then unfold from the SUV, already wishing I'd come up with some sort of excuse.

Might as well get in and get it over with, then I can go home and down the rest of the whiskey I'd been babysitting all week.

If Diana hadn't cornered me, I never would have agreed to take her daughter out on a date. The last thing I want or need is to get tangled up in a relation-ship. No matter what everyone says, time hasn't healed my wounds and I'm not sure I want it to. I don't glance at my phone, but I'm tempted to, even if it's only to pretend to look at the time. Instead, I stuff it in my pocket defiantly and head to the crosswalk toward the restaurant.

Considering how pushy Diana can be, her daughter probably didn't have much say tonight either. We both may as well make the best of an awkward situation.

I haven't been to *Bella Bella Italiano* in over a year. In fact, I've done my best to avoid it. It wasn't until Diana started walking away, after getting me to agree to the date that the name of the restaurant sunk in. Maybe I can convince the hostess to seat us in a quiet, secluded section where we won't be disturbed. Then I can make some chit-chat with Diana's daughter and make some excuse and get out without leading this girl on.

There are a variety of restaurants in Nassau, certainly plenty of Italian joints, but there's already a crowd at the entrance. I sigh as I wait for the traffic to thin so I can cross the street. After spending all day in a crowded emergency room, the only thing I want is the slow burn of alcohol and a dark room where I can brood.

Resigned, I look to my left and right, then up again to make sure the road is clear.

That's when I see her.

The force of my reaction flattens me against the driver's side door, stealing my breath, and damn near stopping my heart. For a second there, I think I may need a trip back to the E.R., then I remember to breathe, though it doesn't unpin me from the car.

I recognize her from the various pictures Diana's flashed from time to time, beaming with pride. I'd known she was beautiful, in a kind of passing sort of way. The way you see a piece of art in a museum from the corner of your eye and appreciate it, but not care about it. In person, she's stunning, which floors me because I haven't even been slightly attracted to a woman in ages.

But it's there, burning low in my stomach, in the heated flow of my blood.

And the attraction is even worse than indifference.

I glance down at the wedding band on my left hand. The one I haven't thought of taking off in the year since I watched the woman I loved wither away from an illness I couldn't cure.

When I look back up, Stella is making her way inside and despite my excuses and grumbling, I find myself following close behind her. Her voice is musical, throaty, and carries over the din of the restaurant conversation and white noise from the kitchen. As the hostess points her to the bar, I nod, not giving her time to ask me where I'd like to sit. For some inexplicable reason, I want to observe Stella first. Need to see her.

Then I'll force myself to get on with the date and quite possibly my life.

She takes a seat at the bar and orders a white wine from the bartender. I navigate through the evening crowd to an empty chair on the opposite side of the bar and wave away the bartender who comes to take my order. Stella sips her wine, bringing the glass to full, red lips and tousling the lush weight of her dark curls.

A pair of women approach behind Stella as she studies her emptying glass, and my heart thuds in my chest when I recognize them as members from The Sanctum.

I give a nod to the bartender and gesture for them to bring me a tumbler of whiskey. Downing it the moment he sets it on the table, I relish the burn as it slides down my throat.

I hadn't been to The Sanctum since Miranda died. Hadn't wanted to see other couples blissed out in the throes of an irreplaceable connection. Hadn't wanted to be reminded of the memories I've spent the past few months trying to forget.

Without thinking, I shoot off a quick text to the number Diana gave me for Stella. I can't do this. Can't be in the place, reminded of all I've lost.

Some things are irreplaceable.

I get to my feet to leave, when I see Stella caught up in conversation with Tally and another Sanctum member. Other patrons flow around me as I come to a stop in the middle of the aisle, watching as Stella follows them down the hall to a private room.

Each step is like walking through cement, but I make it to the open doorway. When I step inside, I'm met with raised brows and twisted lips. Tally notices me and starts to come forward, but I shake my head and move to an empty seat in the corner that will keep me relatively concealed from the group—and Stella in particular.

At Tally's motion, the other regular members of The Sanctum who attend the munches to welcome newcomers also leave me alone. Presumably under the guise of respect for my wife—which only serves to make the guilt burn alongside the whiskey in my stomach.

A man, one I don't recognize, approaches Stella and she stiffens slightly, her eyes going to the floor for the barest of moments, but it's enough for me to stiffen in the confines of my slacks. For the first time in over a year, I want to take a woman. Want to own her.

But not just any woman. This one.

Her dark hair flutters over her shoulders and her smooth creamy skin teases underneath the hem of her dress. I image all those curls spread over her body and nothing else. I imagine holding it in my fists as she kneels before me, those bright red lips glistening for me.

Begging.

She raises her eyes, glancing around the crowd, almost looking to see if anyone is watching and I know, with a certainty that's always served me well in my profession, that she's as addicted to the audience as I am to subservience.

Without giving myself a chance to think about the consequences for the first time in a long time, I send another text to her phone. This time not to drive her away, but to see her again. Without the pulse-pounding addition of The Sanctum members around us.

To see if the needs stirring inside of me are real.

Thankfully, the dinner ends and she bids goodbye to the man sitting next to her. His eyes follow her as she leaves, just as mine do. Her cheeks are red, either from excitement or the growing heat in the crowded room, and her eyes are bright. She draws the eyes of everyone in the room and I wonder if she knows.

She speaks with Tally, who hands her a card. The warmth in my stomach contracts and I have to grip the edge of the table to keep from striding across the room and taking her. I force myself to finish off my tumbler of whiskey, force myself to think of my wife, the woman I loved all during medical school, my residency, my childhood.

I never thought I'd find another woman I'd want to be mine. To shape and mold under my hands and command. When she died, I thought that part of me died with her. God knows the good parts of me did.

Now all that's left are the darkest parts.

I get out my phone again and dial her number. As she leaves the room, I follow a safe distance behind. She brings the phone up to her cheek while pushing the door open to go outside. The line connects, linking us.

"Hello," I say.

Acknowledgments

To my Knockouts for being beside me every step of the way.

To my family, always.

About the Author

 **Nicole Blanchard** is the New York Times and USA Today best-selling author of dangerous romance from antiheroes to aliens. She and her family reside in the Sunshine State along with their menagerie of animals. Nicole is represented by Katie Monson at SBR Media.

Visit her website www.authornicoleblanchard.com for more information or to subscribe to her newsletter for updates on sales and new releases.

Also by Nicole Blanchard

Battleboro Fire & Rescue Series

Storming His Heart

Shielding His Heart

Saving His Heart

First to Fight Series

Anchor

Warrior

Valor

Box Set: Books 1-3

Survivor

Savior

Honor

Box Set: Books 4-6

Traitor

Operator

Aviator

Captor

Dark Romance

Toxic

An Immortal Fairy Tale Series

Deal with the Dragon

Vow to the Vampire

Kiss from the King

Standalone Novellas

Bear with Me

Darkest Desires

Mechanical Hearts